The
Troublesome
Tooth Fairy

Sandi Toksvig

Illustrated by Georgien Overwater

www.booksattransworld.co.uk/childrens

THE TROUBLESOME TOOTH FAIRY
A CORGI PUPS BOOK : 0 552 546631

First publication in Great Britain

PRINTING HISTORY
Corgi Pups edition published 2000

5 7 9 10 8 6 4

Set in Bembo Infant

Corgi Books are published by Transworld Publishers,
61-63 Uxbridge Road, London W5 5SA,
a division of The Random House Group Ltd,
in Australia by Random House Australia (Pty) Ltd,
20 Alfred Street, Milsons Point, Sydney, NSW 2061,
in New Zealand by Random House New Zealand Ltd,
18 Poland Road, Glenfield, Auckland 10,
and in South Africa by Random House (Pty) Ltd,
Endulini, 5A Jubilee Road, Parktown 2193

Made and printed in Great Britain by
Cox & Wyman Ltd, Reading, Berkshire.

CONTENTS

Series Reading Consultant: Prue Goodwin,
Reading and Language Information Centre,
University of Reading

For Jesse, Megan and Ted

Chapter One

Jessica's granny wasn't like other grannies. She never ever wore a shawl or a flowery dress or sensible shoes to help bad feet. In fact, the day Jessica went to see Granny about her tooth,

Granny was wearing a
cowboy outfit. Granny
was in her kitchen but
she wasn't doing granny
things like knitting or
cooking. She was dancing.
It was a Tuesday and Granny
went line dancing on Tuesdays.

"Granny," said Jessica, a bit
excited, "it's happened!"

"That's wonderful," exclaimed
Granny. Then she leant forward
and whispered, "What has?"

Jessica smiled at her. Right in the middle of her mouth was a large gap.

"My tooth has come out!"

Jessica felt in her pocket and pulled out a small piece of tissue paper. Inside was a small but perfect white tooth, which, that morning, had been helping Jessica to eat an apple.

"That's marvellous," declared Granny, doing a short tap dance in her cowboy boots.

"I think this calls for champagne, don't you?"

Jessica nodded. She knew it wasn't real champagne but they had the drink in champagne glasses anyway.

"Are you going to leave it under your pillow?" Granny asked, while she poured the drinks.

Jessica nodded. "Oh, yes. My friend Katie got a pound for her tooth."

"Splendid," beamed Granny, "at last I can tell you."

"Tell me what?" asked Jessica.

Granny put the drinks on the kitchen table and sat down.

"About the troublesome tooth fairy.

I promised to keep it a secret
till I had a grandchild of my
own who lost a tooth." Granny
settled down to her story.

"It happened to me when I
was your age. I had a
troublesome tooth fairy."

"Troublesome? What do you
mean?" asked Jessica, wide-eyed
and toothless.

"Well, it was all rather surprising. I must have been about six, maybe seven.

My tooth came out after a rather nasty fall from an apple tree. To be honest, I was lucky to survive at all."

11

"Because of the fall?"

"No. Because of the tooth fairy. Oh, she was hopeless. A real first-timer." Granny took a sip of pink champagne before she carried on.

"It was the first tooth I had lost. At bedtime my mother wrapped it in a lace handkerchief and placed it under my pillow.

I remember I was so excited
that I lay watching my pillow by
the light of the moon.
But I must have fallen asleep
because, the next thing I knew,
the clock in the hall was striking
four in the morning. I opened my
eyes and saw a shadow at the
window. A small, mysterious
shadow . . ."

Chapter Two

It was the tooth fairy, but it was not the efficient leave-you-your-money-and-take-the-tooth fairy that I was expecting. No, this was a hopeless tooth fairy. A troublesome, trainee tooth fairy.

She was about fifteen centimetres tall and dressed in purple and silver. She looked lovely, but I didn't realize that it was because her tooth fairy outfit was brand-new. You see, she had never been to collect anyone's tooth before. The fairy stood on the window-sill outside my bedroom and muttered to herself.

"Ten Blanford Road . . . ten . . . yes."

The fairy took out a small book. I could just read the title – *Ten Tasks of the Tooth Fairy*.

The tiny creature began reading through some instructions. She had a very high-pitched voice which I could hear quite clearly through the window.

"*First locate the home of the person who has lost his or her tooth.*" The fairy left the windowsill and flew down to check our house number.

In a moment she reappeared on
the window sill. "Yes, ten." She
looked at her book
again.

"*Rule Two —
Enter the said
property.*
Right." The
fairy shut her eyes,
squared her shoulders
and walked straight
at the window.
The bang of her
head on the glass
echoed through
my whole bedroom.

Ow!

"Ow!" she said, so loudly that I was sure Mother would come in at any moment. She shook her head and took her book out again. "*Enter the said property . . . using Tooth Fairy Technique.* Ah, tooth fairy technique. How could I have forgotten?

I must remember to read on properly."

She began to mutter a little poem:

"Tooth Fairy, Tooth Fairy
Be soft and not scary
Enter the house
Quiet as a mouse
Shimmer, now shimmer
Enter with a glimmer."

The tiny creature began to vibrate until she was just a shimmering light, which quietly passed through the window pane and into my room.

Chapter Three

Once she was through the window, the fairy collapsed onto the end of my bed puffing noisily.

"Sssh!" I said, "You'll wake Mother."

"Oh, no, no, no, no," exclaimed the fairy crossly.

"Grown-ups never wake up when the tooth fairy comes. Why, how do you think we would get any work done if . . .?" The fairy stopped for a moment and looked very annoyed.

"You're not supposed to be awake either. That spoils the whole thing. At least I think it does." She frowned and began thumbing through her book again.

I could see a large sign with a
"T" on it pinned to her back.

"What's the 'T' for?" I asked.

"Hmmm?" The fairy was
busy reading.

She looked up for a minute.

"Oh, that, yes, it means
'Trainee'. I'm new, you see. I've
not done a human tooth before.

I've been doing cats and dogs
for a while. I was quite good
apart from
trying to take
a canine from
a Great Dane
who wasn't
ready yet.
You're my first
actual child. Now sssh!" She
went back to her book. "Yes,
here it is. *Rule Number Three –
Check the child is asleep.*" The fairy
snapped her book shut with a
sigh. "Well, you're not asleep,
are you? I suppose I shall have

to come back tomorrow."

The fairy got up, shook herself
and moved towards the window.
She looked miserable.

"Don't go!" I
called. "I tell you
what, I could
pretend to be
asleep. No-one
would know."

"Really?" said the fairy, stopping on the windowsill and having a think. "That would be awfully kind."

"No trouble at all." I shut my eyes and waited for her to get on with taking the tooth.

mutter mutter

I could hear her muttering
to herself.

"Better be quick. Don't want to
get caught. What's the next
thing?" She was obviously in a
hurry because I don't think she
checked her book properly.

"Rule Four . . . can't
remember.
Never mind.
Rule Five.
What is Rule
Five? Oh yes –
take the child," she murmured
and before I knew it something
very odd started to happen.

The fairy chanted:

"*Now fly, fly*
High in the sky
The time is at hand
For Tooth Fairy Land"

Slowly I began to rise above my bed. I knew I wasn't sleeping because I could see my teddy bear on the bed below me.

I could feel myself getting
smaller until I was just as tiny as
my fairy friend. I don't know how
I stayed in the air. The fairy
wasn't holding me.

We floated twice around the
bedroom and then with a
shimmer and a shivery feeling we
flew out of the room. We went
straight through the window
pane as if it wasn't there.

We floated over the front garden,
over the gravel path to the gate,
across the night sky and away.

Chapter Four

If you've never flown through the
night sky in just your pyjamas,
you will never know how thrilling

it is. It was wonderful.
We flew over my
school and the playing
fields. We flew over the
milkman who was just
starting work. We flew
over a pub where the landlord
was asleep on the sofa.

We flew over a house which was having a noisy party. We flew on and on towards the stars. I felt quite safe and  very relaxed even though I was high above the ground. After a  while we flew into a large cloud and very gently we descended through the mist to the ground.

It took a moment for the mist to clear. We appeared to have arrived in a strange new land. A land that was very white and very odd.

At first I couldn't make out what
anything was but the fairy
seemed quite at home.

"This way," she called,
hurrying on ahead of me.

I followed her even though I was
beginning to feel a little anxious.

After a moment I saw a huge
valley below me like a deep,
black hole. It was dark and
scary with lots of broken bits of
white littering the steep sides.

"That's the Valley of No Repair," said the fairy, stopping to look me straight in the eye. "It's full of teeth which haven't been looked after."

A bridge appeared before us. It was pure white and surprisingly strong when you stepped onto it.

Valley of No Repair

WELCOME TO REAL TOOTH LAND
read the sign as we crossed over
to the other side of the valley.

It was an amazing place.
Everything was made of teeth.
Hundreds of fairies were going
about their business.

Lots of them were carrying teeth
or swapping teeth for money at
the bank.

We hadn't gone very far when
suddenly there was a terrible
noise.

"Trainee Twelve!" boomed an incredibly loud voice. Everyone went silent.

TRAINEE TWELVE!

Nothing could be heard except a couple of teeth chattering in someone's arms.

My fairy stopped in her tracks.

"Oh dear, it's the Head Fairy," she said.

A huge fairy, dripping with
bits of gold and silver filling,
stood in front of us.

Four guards stood to attention
behind her.

My trainee looked quite
frightened. The giant reached
out and grabbed my shoulder.

"What, may I ask, is this?"
demanded the fairy.

"Ah," said my trainee. "It's the
child I went to collect . . ."

"Not the child!" screamed the Head Fairy. "The tooth. You're supposed to collect the tooth."

My trainee grabbed her rule book and began to thumb through it. "But it says – *Rule Five – Take the child . . . 's tooth.* Ah . . ." The little fairy blushed.

"I'm so sorry. I . . . uh . . . . .
forgot to read on."

Everyone was watching as
the huge fairy leant forward and
whispered urgently to the
trainee.

"Children are not allowed
here. What have you done?
Now we'll have to get rid of it.
Guards, arrest them both."

Chapter Five

We were both taken to a large room where a lot of fairies had gathered. Everyone seemed most upset. The Head Fairy was ranting, "This is outrageous. Nothing like this has happened since gob-stoppers were invented."

"Oh dear," said my trainee fairy, miserably. She stood in a corner with drooping wings and her head hung low.

Behind a very high desk sat a white-haired old fairy. The guards stood to attention as he spoke.

"Trainee Twelve, you are charged with bringing a child to Tooth Fairy Land, where no child should ever enter. First witness." The old fairy banged a toothbrush on the desk and the guards pushed me forward.

A fairy in a black cloak held out a small mirror in front of my face.

"Say aaah!" said the fairy in
a bored voice.

"Aaah," I said obediently.

The fairy handed me a cup of
pink water.

"Rinse and spit."

I took a sip
of the water
and spat it
out in a
bucket

by my side. "You may proceed,"
said the old fairy.

"Tell us what happened."

"Well," I said. "I was in bed
and then . . ."

The old fairy banged his brush on the desk again and announced, "Just as I thought. Disgraceful. Trainee Twelve, you will be stripped of your wings and never collect another tooth again.

Right, time for tea."
The guards
grabbed my
weeping
trainee and
everyone
started to leave.

"Wait!" I cried.
"What about me?"

There was silence as the old
fairy looked at me. "You, child?"
he said.

"I have to
go home."
He shook
his head.

Wait!

"You can't leave. Tooth Fairy Land is supposed to be secret and now that you've been, you will tell everyone.

"This is very serious."

"Very serious," muttered all the fairies in the court, shaking their heads.

"Look, it wasn't my fault or the trainee's, either. She just wasn't ready for the job." The entire room was silent as I carried on.

"If my mother finds me missing in the morning she will cause a terrible fuss. What if the word got out that one of your tooth fairies made a mistake?

That you had taken a child
instead of a tooth? Why, no
child in the world would ever
trust you with their teeth again.
There would be no more new
teeth in Tooth Fairy Land."

A gasp ran through the fairies.

"Tooth Fairy Land would begin to decay and you could never get another tooth to repair it."

The old fairy looked worried.
"She's right. What can we
do?"

I was rather nervous but I
stood my ground and looked at
them all. "You must agree never

again to send trainees out alone.
I think they need someone to
help them. If you don't agree
then I shall have to tell all the
children that it isn't safe to put
their teeth
under the
pillow."
There
was a
dreadful
silence and
I thought
perhaps I had gone too far. The
toothbrush banged once more
and the old fairy spoke.

"I am ready to announce my verdict. The child is right.

Collecting teeth is a serious business and we should not have sent a young trainee to do a proper fairy's job. In future all trainees will be accompanied by a qualified fairy until they are

ready to take on full teeth-
collecting responsibility.
Trainee Twelve –
you are forgiven
but will undergo
rigorous
re-training."

"And me?" I said.
"Yes, you may
go home but you
must promise to tell
no-one about
this."

"Not ever?"

There was some discussion until the old fairy said, "We realize that it would be a difficult secret to keep for ever so we have decided – you must stay silent until we have had time to ensure such a disaster never happens  again. You may not reveal this 'adventure' for many years. You must wait till you have a grandchild who loses a tooth. If you agree, then you may go home."

I nodded.

All the fairies gathered to see me off. The Head Fairy herself walked with me and my trainee to the bridge over the Valley of No Repair.

Soon the three of us were across the valley and back into the mists. Once again we floated high above the ground. Before I knew it, I was back to normal size and in my bed. The Head Fairy winked at me as she took my tooth and laid a brand new shiny penny in its place . . .

Chapter Six

Granny sighed and finished her champagne. "Thank goodness it all turned out well or I wouldn't be here telling the story."

Jessica looked at her granny who was smiling. "Is that true, Granny?"

Granny grinned. "Things are sometimes true if you believe them." She got up from her chair.

"Let me know whether or not
you get a pound for your tooth."
Jessica went home with the
tooth and put it under her pillow

That night, while Jessica slept,
when the hall clock chimed four
in the morning, there were not

one but two tiny shadows
standing shimmering at her
bedroom window.

THE END